DISNEY
Fairies

PICTURE PERFECT

STORYBOOK AND MYPOD

adapted by Sarah Heller
from an original story by Lisa Papademetriou

illustrated by Judith Holmes Clarke
and the Disney Storybook Artists

Reader's
Digest
Children's Books

Pleasantville, New York • Montréal, Québec • Bath, United Kingdom

PLAY
SONG
1

BESS WHISTLED AS SHE FLEW through the woods. It was a beautiful morning, and Bess was in a wonderful mood.

"Hello, Bess!" Fira called from her spot in a sunny clearing. Fira was a light-talent fairy and she loved to sit in the sunshine. "Where are you off to?"

"I'm headed to my new studio," Bess replied. "I want to make the perfect painting to hang on the wall—something that will inspire me whenever I look at it."

"That sounds like a lot of work!" Fira said.

Bess nodded. "That's why I need peace and quiet," she said. "I have to concentrate."

"Well, good luck!" Fira called as Bess zipped away. Fira settled back, basking in the sun.

"Where is Bess going?" someone asked.

Fira opened one eye. "Oh, hello, Rani," she said. "Bess is off to her new art studio." Fira waved her hand toward the deepest part of the woods. "She said that she needs some inspiration."

"Bess isn't feeling inspired?" Rani asked. She looked concerned.

"She is, but—" Fira started to explain.

But Rani wasn't listening. "I know just what she needs," she said excitedly. "See you later, Fira." With that she hurried off toward Havendish Stream.

PLAY
SONG
3

"It's perfect!" Rani cried as she plucked a smooth stone from the bottom of Havendish Stream.

"What's perfect?" Tinker Bell asked, flying up beside her.

Rani grinned at her friend. "This!" she exclaimed, holding out the stone. "Fira says that Bess needs some inspiration," Rani told Tink. "And I thought, what's more inspiring than a beautiful stone that has been worn smooth by the water? I can't wait for Bess to see it!" With a wave, she hurried off.

"Inspiration, *hmmm!*" Tink murmured to herself. Personally, whenever she needed inspiration, she just looked at the pots in her workshop. "That's it!" Tink cried. "I know just what Bess needs."

PLAY
SONG
4

Moments later, Tink was on her way to Bess' workshop. She struggled to carry a large copper pot.

"Let me help you, Tink," Lily said. "Where are you taking this pot?"

Tink explained that she was taking the pot to Bess to give her some inspiration.

"Inspiration?" Lily said, pausing in midair. "Wait! I need to go back to my garden to get a flower for Bess. My violets are very inspiring."

Tink grumbled—but only a little—as she and Lily flew back to the violet patch. Lily took her time selecting the perfect flower. Then the two fairies dug it up and planted it in Tink's pot.

"Perfect!" Lily cried.

Tink had to agree that the pot and the flower were very inspiring. Even though in her opinion the pot was a little more inspiring.

"Tink! Lily!" Beck called. "Where are you going?"

"We're taking this flower and pot to Bess for inspiration," said Lily.

"H*mmm*," Beck replied, tugging thoughtfully on a strand of hair. "That gives me an idea."

PLAY
SONG
6

Meanwhile, Bess had arrived in the deepest part of the woods. "There it is," she sang, as her brand-new art studio came into view.

Bess' studio was a plain wooden crate that had once been used to hold tangerines. Bess had found it washed up on the shore of Never Land. She had used magic to move it to a very quiet, peaceful part of the woods.

"Now there will be no interruptions," Bess said, as she flew into the studio. "No distractions," she added, looking at the blank walls. "I can paint in peace all day."

15

PLAY
SONG
7

Bess sat down and tried to paint, but nothing came to her mind. So she tried flying upside down. "This isn't working either," she said. She had thought that standing on her head would give her an idea. But now she just felt dizzy.

She righted herself. "Maybe if I sing something..." Bess mused. She launched into the first verse of her favorite song, but her voice trailed off before she got to the chorus. She felt very silly singing to an easel.

Bess tried meditating, yelling, reciting fairy history, covering her eyes with a fern frond, counting to one hundred, and pretending not to care. Nothing worked.

♪
PLAY
SONG
8

"Oh!" Bess cried. "Why can't I think of anything?"

Finally, Bess fell flat on her back. She stared up at the ceiling. "I'm not going to move until I get an idea," she said.

"Knock, knock!" someone sang.

Bess turned her head.

A face peeked into the studio. "It's me, Fira! How's your painting going? Why are you lying on the floor?"

"I'm fine," Bess said. "I'm just trying to get some work done." Then she hustled Fira out the door.

"Hello!" cried a friendly voice. Bess looked and saw Tink and Lily hovering overhead.

More visitors. Bess sighed.

"We brought you a present," Lily said.

"The pot's from me," Tink said.

"And I brought the flower," said Lily.

At that moment, Beck and Rani stepped out of the woods.

"I've brought you a present!" Rani said. She held out her river stone. "For inspiration."

"I brought something, too!" Beck said. She held out two eggshells. "You can use these to mix paints," she said.

Bess accepted the gifts. *These gifts are wonderful,* she thought. *But I wish everyone would just go away. How can I work?*

Grabbing her largest brush, Bess darted over to the long wall of her studio and started to paint. The other fairies watched, amazed, as a painting began to appear before them.

Finally, just as the sun was dipping below the trees, Bess stood back to look at her work. On the wall, she had painted her five friends—all of them smiling.

"What a beautiful picture!" Lily said.

"I like the way you put our presents in the background," Beck added.

"The pot looks especially nice," Tinker Bell pointed out.

Bess put one arm around Fira and the other around Rani and grinned. "Now, if that isn't an inspired painting," she said to her friends, "I don't know what is."